Hit Like a Girl

Keith Wheeler

Hit Like a Girl

is just the beginning.

Get a sneak peek at

Chapter One from

One Bad Call!

www.kwheelerbooks.com/onebadcall

DEDICATION

This story is dedicated to all the hard-working softball players out there. Enjoy the ride!.

"Cam, don't worry. We know you'll do great!" The look on her mom's face was already beaming with pride and excitement and Cam hadn't even gotten out of the car yet. Well, it was really a minivan: the go-to vehicle for a family who spends more time traveling to and from softball games than family vacations.

"I don't know Mom. This is high school softball. There's a lot more competition than there was at the junior high." Cam's voice trembled a bit as she said the words, '*High School*'. She still couldn't believe she was there. Somehow, she was supposed to battle for a spot on a team that already had so many great players. The more she thought about it, the more she wanted to just forget the whole thing.

"I can just play travel ball. I don't need to play at the high school too."

"Cam Dixon… Get your butt out there and just do your best. You'll do great!" Her mom was a bit more forceful this time. She always had a way of sounding sweet even when making Cam do something terrifying.

Cam barely got her bag and cleats out of the back of the van when she heard some of the other girls start walking to the field. The unmistakable sound of metal cleats hitting the cement walkway helped relax her a bit as she slipped on her cleats and headed to the field.

This was crazy! She only recognized a few girls. Where did the rest of them come from? Since there was only one junior high in their town, Cam figured she'd know most, if not all, of the girls there. She was clearly mistaken. As expected, there were the girls that played for the high school the previous year, but it was the number of incoming freshman that really surprised her. To top it off, there were quite a few girls that looked much older, perhaps sophomores or juniors, that were NOT on the team last year. *Could they all be transfer students?*

She felt a slight sense of relief as her best friend, Roxie, started heading her way, cleats in hand. "I think I'm gonna throw up!" Cam told Roxie, acid building up in her throat.

"There sure are a crap load of new girls, huh Cam?" Roxie always had an eloquent way of putting things. That's probably why they got along so well. Roxie had no problem saying exactly what Cam was thinking.

"There sure are. Those girls look way older than 9th grade. I don't even recognize half of these incoming freshman. They didn't all go to school with us last year, did they?" Cam's palms started to sweat, which made it even harder to put her glove on.

"I don't know Cam. All I know is that you and I belong on this team. Let's show these newbies how it's done!" Luckily for Cam, Roxie had enough confidence for them both.

"Let's go ladies. Start warming up." Coach Johnson's booming voice reminded them of why they were there. This wasn't a social event; this was business.

Hearing his voice helped Cam relax a bit. She'd been to enough high school softball games that she felt like she already knew him.

Okay Cam... This is why you're here. Just do what you know and you'll be fine. Oh yeah...and don't suck!

"Dixon...go cover first and let's see what you've got." Cam looked around. Where was this 'Dixon' chick? If she didn't show up, it'd be one less girl to compete with. Sweet. A smile began to spread across her face.

"Cam!" Roxie whispered as her elbow gently nudged Cam's ribcage.

Oh right...he's calling out last names. What a great way to start things out, dummy.

"Sorry, Coach, I'm here."

"Okay, head to first and let's see what you've got." Coach Johnson didn't sound annoyed but clearly had a sense of urgency in his voice.

He stood back and hit a decent grounder straight towards first base. Cam stared the ball down, trying to time her charging of the ball to ensure she'd have enough time to quickly tag first as well.

The ball was a blur. Cam charged it, put her glove down, scooped it up, and with just two steps, tagged first base.

"That was an easy one," he said. "Now that I've got you warmed up, let's see what you've really got." He smirked. With just one glance, she could tell this was going to be just as hard as she had feared... maybe worse.

Crack! The next ball flew towards second. She quickly shifted her weight to her right foot lunging sideways. Her goal was to at least stop the ball. *Keep it in the infield!* She could still hear her travel ball coach in her ear.

She remembered back to how hard she'd worked this past season on her dives. She couldn't believe how hard it was for her mind to convince her body to just do it. She could dive back while running bases but for some reason diving to stop a ball was a completely different story. She smiled. Her hard work had finally paid off.

The next two hits snaked to her left. She backhanded one, but the other slipped passed her glove. He finished up the round with another hit to her right side. Once again, she shifted her weight and dove for the ball. As she reached for the ball it grazed her pinkie and continued to fly into right field.

Crap!

"Next!" Coach yelled.

Cam couldn't tell if that was urgency or aggravation in his voice. It took everything she had to not break down and cry right then.

Cam ripped her glove off and started heading back to the dugout. She blew her shot. What coach would want a player that can only stop a ball three out of five times?

"Where are you going?" Roxie's voiced seemed sincerely confused.

"Where do you think? I just blew it! There's no sense in me wasting any more time here. I'll just stick with travel ball."

"Oh, right. I forgot you're perfect in travel ball, right? Yeah, never make an error or have a bad day. My bad, you're right. Have a nice day." It's been a long time since Roxie had to pull out the 'tough love' voice. Cam knew she was right. She was far from a perfect softball player. She'd made plenty of errors in travel ball, but also had some really, amazing days, too.

"I get it, Roxie," Cam said as she put her glove back on. She couldn't help but notice the smirk on Roxie's face. She just loved it when she was right. Mama Roxie was right again! It would be a while before Roxie would forget about this one.

"Hey Rox, wipe your face, you've got a little sarcasm right there." Cam smiled as she gently poked Roxie's lower lip. The smirk on Roxie's face grew bigger when she saw the playful side of her best friend reemerge.

They watched as the rest of the girls tried out for their respective positions. She paid especially close attention to those girls trying out for the corners. First and Third were 'her' spots. Sure, she'd played other positions, but those were where she really felt at home.

Some of the girls were really, good. Most of the girls that were returning from last year were amazing. Although there were a few who seemed like they had gotten a little rusty over the off season. Perhaps Cam still had a shot to make the team, after all.

"Ok ladies. Why don't you go get a drink and then we'll start working on some hitting?" As all the girls headed back to their bat bags to devour their water bottles and prepare for hitting, Coach Johnson headed over to the other dugout and pulled out a screen that was in the shape of an "L" and started warming up his pitching arm.

"Hey Cam, I think we've got a real shot at making the team, don't you?" Of course, Roxie had a shot, she was an amazing ball player. The only part that really frustrated Cam was how easy it came to her. She hardly ever practiced and yet, was a ball magnet, both offensively and defensively. This was the exact opposite of Cam. She loved softball and spent every moment she could, playing and practicing, trying everything she could to get better. To get, in her mind; *as good as Roxie!*

"Oh, just great… now we've got company." You could hear the venom in Cam's voice as she spat the words out. She hated it when the boys would come 'watch' the softball tryouts.

"Oh my god, girls. I think those boys are coming over to check us out." Tara was so clueless. She's the type of girl that makes everyone else think that all freshman girls are airheads.

"Do you really think so, T?" you could feel the eagerness in Jessica's voice as she stared at her best friend for confirmation.

Cam wasn't sure which irritated her more; the fact that the boys were coming over to watch them or the notion that these potential teammates of hers actually thought that was why the boys were coming over.

Cam knew better. She knew from experience the only reason why a group of teenage boys would come over to watch girls try out for softball was to make fun of them.

"Man, that aggravates the crap out of me, Rox," her face growing redder by the moment.

"Oh, it'll be fine, Cam. Don't let them get in your head." Roxie knew exactly how her best friend played when she was irritated or distracted and was adamant that she was not going to let Cam sabotage herself by giving in to those emotions. The last thing she wanted was for Cam to not make the team, all because of a few stupid, hormone-driven, immature boys.

"Just go out there, Cam, and hit the crap out of the ball!" Roxie tried to redirect Cam's frustration and channel it into something useful.

"Or better yet, pretend the ball is the face of one of the boys up there." As Roxie pointed in the direction of the boys, a huge, sinister smile slithered across her face.

"Oh, hell yeah! That's a beautiful idea, Rox. You sure do know how to cheer me up!" All the nerves and anxiety Cam was feeling quickly melted away. In its place was almost an electricity. She didn't know how to describe it, but all her muscles were screaming at her, begging to be able to release their energy out onto the ball.

"Let's do this!" Cam's smile disappeared as quickly as it came, leaving nothing but the most serious look Roxie had ever seen before. It reminded her of the look her dad had when he was negotiating a deal on her mom's last car. So, serious; it was almost scary.

"Okay ladies, who's first?" The sound of Coach Johnson's voice shocked Cam and Roxie back to reality. Though he'd asked who was first, everyone knew that the returning girls would always be the first to hit. Cam never really understood why...

They know they've made the team already! Just the thought irritated Cam. *Just because they were good enough last year, doesn't mean they're good enough this year.*

It came as no shock to Cam when the incoming seniors crushed the ball. They clearly play year-round and practice at home. Cam hoped that would be her in just a few years. With the amount of time and energy she put into the sport, it would just have to pay off, wouldn't it?

Shortly after the returning seniors finished and the juniors began to grab their bats, Coach interrupted, "Hold up ladies. I know we normally have all of the returning girls hit first, but let's mix things up a bit, shall we?" Cam couldn't believe her ears, did Coach really, just say that? If the returners weren't going to hit next, who was?

"How 'bout we jump over to some of these incoming freshmen? What do ya say?" The smile on Coach Johnson's face was almost playful. Like he was intentionally throwing a monkey wrench into the works, just to see the freshmen squirm.

"So, who wants the first shot at hitting off the old man?" *Old man? This guy can't be much older than my dad. If I called my dad an old man he'd whoop my a...*

"Dixon...how about you? You ready to take a few swings?" The electricity that was pumping through Cam's veins just moments earlier, quickly transformed into millions of butterflies bombarding her stomach.

She nonchalantly leaned to Roxie and muttered, "I think I'm gonna throw up!" Those butterflies were sure working hard, generating so much energy that Cam could feel the acid rising up in her throat.

"Relax, Cam. You got this, remember?" Roxie's barely audible response was muffled even more through her clenched smile. She didn't want Coach to see them chatting, but she had to pump up her bff. "Their face is the ball. Their face is the ball!" Using just her eyes, Roxie pointed at the boys sitting in the bleachers.

Cam knew she was right, Roxie was always right. All Cam had to do was focus on the ball and hit it. Imagining the ball was their face, was just an added bonus.

"Can I go first, Coach?" Cam was startled when she heard Roxie chime in. Leave it to Roxie to find a way to give her friend a few more minutes to 'get in the zone' before she had to hit. And what guts! To go up to bat right after those seniors crushed it? The confidence! But, of course, Roxie had confidence, she knew she had the skills to back it up.

Cam didn't realize she'd been standing there, mouth wide open, just admiring her best friend's ability to smash the ball, until she heard one of the boys from the bleachers yell, "I think you're drooling a little there, princess."

She could hear their cackling and not-so-quite snarky comments, which only refueled her anger from before. As Roxie headed back to the dugout, Cam turned to her and grunted, "Boys should not be allowed to come and watch our tryouts!"

"Remember what we talked about, Cam. Just take it out on the ball!" She knew Roxie was right, but the sound of the boys continued to enrage her. She'd deduced that the loudest boy, who was about 6 inches taller than the rest of his group, must be the leader of the idiot-brigade.

"Show them how it's done, Cam." Roxie's words of encouragement helped calm her down as Cam stepped up to the plate.

"You ready Dixon?"

"Ready, Coach." She wasn't sure why she kept calling him Coach, technically he wasn't her coach yet. Not until she, actually, made the team.

If I make the team. That voice of doubt kept creeping back. She tried pushing it out of her head, but there it was. Like the carrot sticks her mom insisted on putting in her lunch, she could not get rid of that doubt.

She didn't even notice Coach wind up to pitch the first ball at her. She was a bit surprised at the speed he was throwing it. Based on the wind that she felt, as the strike flew by her, he must have been throwing it around 50-55 mph. Not too shabby for a self-proclaimed 'Old Man'!

She could hear the boys snickering behind her as she felt the tears begin to well up. *Don't cry, don't cry!*

"You ok, Dixon?"

"Yeah, sorry Coach. I just zoned out for a minute. I'm ready."

"Ok, I'll give you 3 more pitches." That was fair. Everyone else was getting 4 pitches and why should he treat her any different just because she completely missed a perfect strike?

Here we go...

The next pitch he threw was toward the inside, just barely hugging the plate. Cam watched as it raced towards her. *What did Dad teach you? That's it, let it travel and hit it to the opposite side.* As the ball got closer, she shifted her weight, rotated her hips and just as the ball reached her back hip, she threw her hands forward and *Whack!* The ball flew over the first baseman's head, just beyond her reach.

"Nice Duck Fart, Cam." Roxie loved those kinds of hits. Not only do they usually result in the batter getting a single, but she really, just loved saying, 'Duck fart'.

"Nice hit Dixon."

"Thanks, Coach."

"Oh, look I'm a girl. I can't hit too hard, I might break a nail." The jerk-prince was really getting on Cam's last nerve. At this point he wasn't even trying to be quiet. She didn't know which angered her more, his loud mouth or the fact that Coach was letting him carry on that way.

"Focus, Cam, you got this." *Roxie's right. Focus, focus.*

Coach wound up. *Watch his hands, watch the spin on the ball.* The ball left his hands much faster than his last pitch. Just as the ball was about half-way to the plate, Cam heard the coach yell, "Bunt third!"

Crap!

Suddenly, all her travel coach's words came rushing at her. *Square up…Bend at the knees…Slight angle…Don't jab at it…annnnd PUSH!*

"Nice bunt, Cam!" Roxie was more excited than she was. Cam just stared as the ball pirouetted, dead center between third and home plate.

"Wow, that was some quick-thinking, Dixon. Not too

shabby." While his words spoke of being impressed, his tone made it clear, he wasn't quite done yet. "Last pitch!" He grabbed another ball from the bucket, pulled back his arm and began his pitch.

The anxiety continued to rise-up in Cam. *This is it Cam. Last pitch. Make it count. You've got this. You've got thi…*

"Don't choke!" The boy sneered, much louder this time.

I hate that kid. Wait, focus, Cam.

The split-second it took her to focus on the boy's outburst was enough time for the ball to get just 4 feet from the plate. With hands higher than normal, Cam brought the knob of the bat straight towards the ball. Then, with a flick of the wrist, she caught the meat of the bat with the center of the ball and sent it screaming to centerfield.

Most of the freshmen girls just stopped and stared as the ball reached the middle of centerfield before dropping. "Nice hit!" a few of them shouted, while the others just stood there, still registering what they'd just witnessed.

"You gentlemen can leave, RIGHT NOW!"

Now, THAT was the reaction Cam was hoping for from the coach. A bit later than she would've liked, but at least they wouldn't be there to harass the rest of the girls.

"That was bull crap, Cam. But what a sweet hit! You pretended it was his face, didn't you?"

"You're darn right I did. Take that, you little punk!" Eventhough she was talking to Roxie, Cam's daggers were fixed on the boy, as he reluctantly left the bleachers. The truth was, Cam didn't pretend it was that jerk's face. She didn't have time. She knew she'd just gotten lucky that she was able to make good contact after that huge distraction. This miss could've cost her the try out.

"Seriously, Rox. Had I missed that ball, I'd have been done. I already missed the first pitch. This is only a one day try out. He really could've screwed me!" Cam was more furious than she could ever remember being before.

"It's fine though. You showed him. You didn't let him get to you. Great job." But she had, let him get to her. She just didn't know why.

"Next…" Coach's voice once again brought Cam back to reality. She put her glove back on and headed to the outfield to help shag balls. Now that the boys were gone, she was actually able to enjoy herself. Softball was her greatest passion and she decided that she wasn't going to let those jerks ruin the rest of the tryout for her.

Most of the girls hit as Cam had expected, although there were one or two surprises. The red-haired girl from her English class last year that talked about softball all the time, couldn't hit the broad side of a barn. While that quiet girl who looked like she weighed 90 lbs soaking wet, could really hit.

"I will call each of you tonight and let you know my decision. You all did great and should be really proud of yourselves, no matter what."

"Thanks Coach" they all said in unison.

As Roxie and Cam started packing their bat bags to leave, Coach Johnson approached them. "Hey ladies. I just wanted to assure you that you both made the team. I was really impressed with your hitting and fielding Roxie."

"Thanks Coach." Roxie looked like she'd just won the lottery.

"Dixon, can I talk to you for a second?"

"Of course, Coach." Her voice cracked just slightly. She'd already made the team so what more could he have to say to her and why was she so nervous?

"Look, I just wanted to apologize for the way those boys were behaving. None of you girls deserved that and I'm sorry I didn't do something about it sooner. But I will say, I'm very impressed with how well you held your own even with that distraction. Very impressive!" With the pride that he exuded you would've thought Cam was his kid.

"Thanks Coach."

"No problem. Have a good night ladies." He said as he turned back to the field to start the arduous job of cleaning up.

"That's so awesome, isn't it Roxie?"

"It sure is. Now, let's head to the parking lot before Coach puts us to work!" the smile on her face made it appear that she was joking, but Cam knew all too well, Roxie was dead serious. She loved Roxie, but her best friend was the laziest person she'd ever met. Roxie would braggingly say that the only thing in the world she was allergic to, was work.

Since Roxie only lived a few blocks away, they decided to take the shortcut to the parking lot by going behind the bleachers. It made the walk home even shorter for Roxie and Cam didn't care, as long as she got to hang out a little while longer with her bff.

This was the happiest either of them had been in a long time. They would be playing together again, in the sport they both loved. They were still giggling and reminiscing about the tryout, as they rounded the back fence.

"Oh, lookie who it is, boys, hello miss princess." His voice was even more annoying when she was facing him. Cam could feel the heat rising back up inside her. All she could think about was that this little punk almost cost her the spot on the high school softball team. How dare he stick around. And why did he seem to focus most of his hostility towards her?

"I really loved that first pitch that you just watch go by you...did it go too fast for you?" he pouted his lips as he said it as if to imitate a toddler about to cry.

Roxie could see how upset Cam was getting, which only made Roxie angrier. She was very protective of her friends, especially when her best friend is being ridiculed by a 14-year-old Neanderthal.

"Oh, am I upsetting you?" his voice got more condescending the more he spoke. His pals chuckled in the background.

"Shut-up!" Roxie said as she saw Cam's face get redder than she thought was humanly possible.

"I'm sorry, but you can't really expect us to take you seriously when you play a 'sport' that actually uses the phrase 'Duck Fart'" Air quotes around the word "sport" enraged the girls even further. The more he carried on, the louder his friends laughed.

"I'm warning you." Roxie said, as she got even closer to her adversary. The only thing standing between the two of them was Cam. Out of the corner of her eye, Roxie noticed a single tear roll down her friend's face. That was the last straw.

He leaned in a bit closer. "Do you know why they call that hit you made a 'Duck Fart'? Because it STUNK!"

WHAP!

Cam looked at Roxie in disbelief. She then looked at the boy who just moments before was harassing her, now lying on the ground clutching his nose. He was doing his best to keep the blood from getting on his white t-shirt. The next place Cam looked, was down at her right hand. It didn't hurt nearly as bad as she expected. She'd never punched anyone before in her life, except her little brother, Stephen, but that was different.

"We're gonna tell the coach and get you thrown off the team!" One of the boys finally muttered; a little frightened of what that threat might mean for him and his face.

"Go ahead," Roxie retorted. "Let the whole school know your friend got beat up by a softball player, I dare ya."

"No, don't!" The boy on the ground moaned, through his cupped hands.

"Cam, your mom's here.", a sudden sense of urgency in Roxie's voice.

"Head home, Rox. I've got this. I'll call you tonight."

"You sure?"

"Yeah," Cam confirmed. "I'm good."

With that, Roxie cut through some backyards and was half-way home in mere seconds. As Cam turned around she saw her mom slowly approaching.

With a new sense of self-confidence, she turned to the boy who threatened to tell Coach on her and asked, "Since your friend is a little busy right now, I'll ask you; what's the little punk's name?"

"Uh...B-Brock, His name is Brock." The boy whimpered.

"Hey Brock," she said, as she turned her attention back to her victim. "I guess now you know how hard a girl can really hit. Oh, and don't worry, I didn't break a nail!" Cam whipped her hair around as she pivoted to turn and head towards her mother's van.

She had a smile from ear to ear as she approached the vehicle and put her bag in the back. As she climbed into the front seat and closed the door, her mom turned to her and asked, "Is everything ok?"

"Everything's great mom.", the smile on her face increasing as they pulled away. "So... how did tryouts go?", though she felt her daughter's smile gave away the answer.

"They went really well, Mom.", Cam responded.

"I Hit Like a Girl!"

Continue the journey with Cam and Roxie.

Sign-up for your exclusive copy of Chapter One of

One Bad Call!

www.kwheelerbooks.com/ONEBADCALL

Made in the USA
Monee, IL
31 October 2019